Ya must have a million
questions. I mean, ya ain't gonna
walk all them stairs just to make
small talk, now are ya.

Tobias Amijo!
All The Best...

LIVING WITH

THE NEW YORK CITY

LIGHTHOUSE KEEPER

by

Tobias Inigo

CHAPTER 1

It's Lonely at The Top

Hey, how ya doin'? What a surprise. I mean, nobody but nobody comes to see me these days. Did ya take the elevator? Ya didn't walk up all those stairs, did ya? Damn, take a seat and I'll get ya a drink. Coffee, tea ... maybe a beer? What's that? A bit too early for ya. I s'pose you're right. Coffee then, eh?

Anyway, ya must have a million questions. I mean, ya ain't gonna walk all them stairs just to make small talk, now are ya.

My name? Good question but kinda predictable if ya don't mind me sayin'. I been called everything ya can think of and then some. It don't really matter to me though, ya see. I mean, names as such ain't that important. Some folks call me a Guiding Light, others

5

think I'm their salvation and call me some real ass-kissin' kinda names. Makes no difference to me.

The ones who really get me are them who don't really ever think of me at all unless they've really got their backs against the wall. Then it's *Master-this* or *All-powerful-that*. Sure it bothers me, even though I can see right through it. I wouldn't be doin' my job looking after all of ya's if I didn't know who needed help and who didn't. One thing I can tell ya for sure, I ain't one for holdin' a grudge. If that was the case, you'd all have been recalled to the factory a long time ago. Still, I do what I can to keep folks out'a trouble and travelin' in the light of this here beacon. The big ones, small ones, rich ones and poor. Makes no difference to me how ya run your lives; good, bad or in-between.

Whaddaya think livin' in the City's for?

Yea ... that's right, you got the idea. Makin' mistakes and tryin' the best ya can to get things movin'. Oh yea, don't forget about bein' happy; that's the most important thing. I know it might seem pretty obvious to ya but it's still the one most of ya get wrong.

Ya see, not everyone wants to know. Maybe you're one of 'em but I don't think so. Ya wouldn't be here if ya were, now would ya. Hey, I understand that some folks gotta do things their own way, even if it gets 'em all screwed up and miserable.

Oh, sure, I'd like to see everyone happy but no-can-do. That's the way the City was designed. It just wouldn't be fair otherwise. Ya gotta understand one thing; if ya don't pay attention and read the signs you're gonna get lost and you're gonna feel helpless.

Whaddaya mean, don't it make me feel kinda bad and unappreciated? 'Course it does but don't get me started on that crap or I'll end up soundin' like your mother.

Of course I care, I wouldn't be here if I didn't, would I. I know it seems like I ain't maybe payin' attention sometimes but that ain't my fault. I'm on the job 'round the clock and I don't get no break or work on flexi-time neither. Just 'cause you see all this high-tech equipment all over the place don't mean things run themselves. If I had a Union Boss I'd prob'ly complain or strike for better conditions ... but I don't - and I won't.

So, would I be here if I didn't care? I ask ya, would I? And it ain't just them in the City I gotta worry about neither.

Take this morning for example; I hadn't even had a cuppa coffee yet. Buddha stops by all stressed out and worried, as usual. He comes bargin' in huffin' and puffin' from climbin' all them stairs. He needed to talk.

Look, I says, *sit down before ya' have a stroke. Ya know, ya should really think about losin' some weight.* He's a big guy, ya see and not so young anymore. Anyway, Buddha sits down on the sofa over there and lights a big Havana cigar. After about two or three beers, he calms down and opens up.

Don't talk to me about losin' weight, he says, his round cheeks all shiny and crimson. *There's a lot more to me bein' fat than meets the eye. Most of this poundage is the weight of other people's problems, not mine. Problems they expect me to deal with.* He takes a long slow coupl'a puffs from his cigar, belches and carries on. *What are all them teachings I left behind anyway, chopped liver? Whatever I was s'pose to do, I've done already.* He shakes his head and sighs. I thought he looked tired. *For Chrisake, I'm supposed to be enjoyin' my retirement!* I just laugh and hand him another beer.

Speakin' of Christ, I says, *he was askin' about ya just the other day.*

Really? Buddha says, *Prob'ly hopin' I'd forgiven him for stealin' most of my ideas is more like it.*

Whoa! Hang on a minute there, big guy. I say and look him straight in the third eye. *Your problems are small compared to his. I mean, a lot of them folks in the City are doin' their damnedest to get your followers to forget everything they believe and follow old JC instead.* Then I laugh to keep things on the light side. *Okay, so he ain't puttin' on the same kinda weight as you but if he has to carry much more guilt around on his shoulders he ain't gonna be able to walk. Ya think he's happy with the way things turned out? Take my word for it, 'cause ya know I don't lie, he ain't.*

Buddha smiles a secret kind'a smile. *I tried to tell him that the crucifixion gag wasn't gonna fix anything. But would he listen to me? Hell no.*

Well, be that as it may, I'll tell ya like I told him. *You guys have helped me' - all of ya's: Jesus, Mohammed, Osiris, Zeus ... every goddamn one-a-ya's are worth your weight in gold. You did good ... so stop worryin'. Just 'cause the City looks like a big mess don't mean we failed. All things considered, it's a damn fine creation and I love it.*

Well, I gotta help Buddha off the couch then. He's had a few too many and he's startin' to get all tearful, the way ya do when ya got a belly full of brew talkin'.

I walk him over to the door, makin' sure he don't trip on the furniture or nothin', and I tell him, *Just keep remindin' yourself, that everybody is born to be happy. It ain't*

your fault if folks hit the rocks now and then 'cause they took a

wrong turn or tried goin' against their natural flow. Hell, even if

they do go belly-up I got more lifeboats than I know what to do

with. There ain't nobody in that City, no matter how crappy it

seems, who ever needs to go under or give up. Buddha smiles

and I think he's feelin' better. *Ya worry too much. Don't*

forget that's a democracy down there. We all got FREE WILL

to contend with and that's some hard nut to crack, as you know.

Maybe it was a bad idea but I don't think so. I mean, so long as

folks have Free Will there'll always be somethin' new happenin' -

somethin' fresh and wonderful. Hell, they even surprise me

sometimes and, believe me, that ain't easy!

Buddha tries to shake my hand but I stop him

and kiss him on both cheeks. *You've already done more than enough so stop feelin' pressured.* I watch him weavin' his way down the hall and I calls out. *Hey, take the elevator this time, ya understand. That's an order!*

Good old Buddha. Folks come and go so quickly where his teachings are concerned. It's 'cause he's just too good natured. I keep tellin' him, ya gotta know when to let go. S'pose if he ever really did listen to me I'd be disappointed, ya know what I mean? Anyway, that's what I told him and that's what I'm tellin' you.

I'm here, in this lighthouse, day in and day out. It isn't just any ol' lighthouse neither, ya understand. It shines in all directions, all the time, and can pick out even the tiniest little critter walkin' under someone's shoe just about ta be squashed, or a whole civilization in a similar quandary, ya know. Still, just the same, even with all that power, it blows my mind the way folks manage to go out of their way walkin' in the dark. Ya see, there's only one problem with usin' this here lighthouse to help folks navigate; it only really shows them the way when they're goin' to places that are gonna' make them happy. Hell, even the worst shit-on-a-shoe rocky road is gonna' be brighter than a smooth and easy one if it's the way you gotta travel to get where ya need to be. Understand? You will.

It's like this; even doin' everything I can, which is a lot, I just can't help those who get lost intentionally; on purpose like. I don't worry about them, though. I mean, ya got free will, emotions, and more than just a pinch of common sense but you all still don't trust your own feelings. When ya don't trust yourself there ain't no way you can trust me. Ya gotta let it flow. If it don't make ya happy then don't do it. Now, d'ya understand? No? Alright then, I'll give ya an example. This is a true story and I know stuff like this happens every day but this one just happens to come ta mind so I'll tell ya.

It was a few years ago now, two maybe five, I think. Ya see, I gotta problem with time and clocks and stuff like that. I can't really squeeze my brain into your way of measurin' things, but anyway, I digress.

Her name was Livvy and she was livin' upstate, away from all the noise and congestion. She'd managed to marry herself a real big earner, a doctor. By most folk's standards, she was on Easy Street but was she happy? Hell no and I'll tell ya why.

CHAPTER 2

Livvy

It all started when she was born … but the whole nut of the problem went back to her grandparents who'd immigrated from a poor, hard life in Russia. They swore that their children and children's children would never have to know that kind of poverty.

Anyway, like I was sayin', it started when she was born. Her parents hadn't been married long and her mother had captured herself a nice young Jewish dentist. So, they were startin' life off on the right foot and keepin' things kosher from the word 'go'.

Well, here's Livvy's mother in Mount Sinai Hospital countin' congratulations cards on the bedside table and waitin' for her young husband, Hershel, to arrive for visitin' time. Livvy was just a day old and,

already, her mother was playin' matchmaker, thinkin'
about the Jewish boy babies which had recently been
born to acquaintances she knew of.

Poor kid, she didn't stand a chance. That's what
ya did when you were a girl and particularly when ya
were a Jewish girl. Ya got married to a doctor or a
dentist or a lawyer and ya had little Jewish babies; boys
preferably but a girl? That was okay too, so long as
they married the right boy and kept to the faith.

Now Livvy wasn't ever really too keen on the
idea of marriage and even less on motherhood. She
just wanted to paint; ya know, be an artist. When she
was at school, winnin' prizes for her artistic

achievements, that was fine; it was just a hobby, a bit of harmless fun.

Every girl needs a hobby, her mother always said, *and what a useful talent it will be when the time comes to marry and buy a house. Oi, the way she can put colors together! She will have no trouble matching up curtains to wallpaper and wallpaper to carpets. What a house she'll have; an absolute palace!*

The poor kid. Not only did she want to go to college and study art but she wanted to marry Steve, a white middle-class gentile boy who she'd had sex with in the back of a '77 Chevy Impala on the night of the school prom when, I hasten to add, she managed to give her Jewish boyfriend, Stanley, the slip by pretendin' to have a headache caused by her period comin' on. Clever girl, but not clever enough.

Stanley, good old considerate and horny Stanley, he only stops by on his way home to see if Livvy had gotten back okay and explain to the parents that she had insisted on takin' a taxi so as not to spoil his evening.

Well, the rest, as they say, is history and happens all the time. The girl is forced to marry Stanley, a man she does not like and practically hates. But who would have her, now that she was no longer a certified virgin?

Anyway, they get married to the tune of twenty-thousand dollars and live with Mr. and Mrs. Finkelstein while their son-in-law finishes medical school, takes his exams and finds himself a tasty little practice in the Big Apple.

Livvy, on the other hand, has not forgotten Steve and has certainly not settled just outside the city, practically New Jersey.

While all of this confusion is goin' on, I am finding it particularly difficult to keep my light shinin' on dear Livvy. Ya see, she is not trustin' her own self and that means she cannot trust me.

Well, all was not lost. As the months go by she is gettin' more and more pressure from Stanley's parents, and her own, to have some nice Jewish babies and make the four of them grandparents.

Just look at that figure! Mrs. Finkelstein would exclaim. *My goil, you are blessed with child-bearing hips if ever I saw them.*

Livvy was not at all sure how much more she could deal with. She was unhappy in the extreme and knew in her heart what she needed to do. So, cutting a long story short, she makes an application to the art school in the city and also arranges an assignation with Steven O'Malley, the very same boy who'd deflowered her in the back of his '77 Chevy Impala and, fortunately for Livvy, was still carryin' a torch himself.

Now, as all this mental sortin' out is going on and Livvy has made some major life decisions whereby she is findin' things impossible not to act upon, I sees her comin' back into the light which has been searchin' for her the whole time from the top of my nine hundred and ninety-seven story Lighthouse-cum-apartment building complex and she is grinnin' from ear to ear. For Livvy, this is the light at the end of the tunnel, so to speak. It is then that I turn up the power and send out a little of the old morse-code: MESSAGE RECEIVED ... HELP ON THE WAY. Ya see, it was only when she was once more on the right track that I could step in and give the poor kid some serious help. That's all there was to it, although I'll be the first to admit, things ain't always so cut and dried. In Livvy's case, she made her choice early on and did not get so lost as others sometimes do. Believe me, some folks get so lost and in so deep I wonder that I ever manage to find 'em again.

CHAPTER 3

Ben

Ben, Ben, Ben. I wonder how many lives he'd have taken if he hadn't gotten help when he did?

He was a safe enough lookin' guy but liked to murder people and women in particular. He was prob'ly what you'd call a serial killer. I just called him *lost*.

Now, before ya start goin' all righteous on me, remember that most of ya don't never see the whole picture, just snatches of it, ya know? So, like I said, Ben had this thing about killin' women and any sort would do, except for fat ones because he was weak and on the small side so fat women were mostly too strong for him and would probably put up a good fight.

Ben hated fightin' and struggle. His life had been full of more than he could deal with already. Murder was a kind of release for Ben and because he was weak and hated that part of himself so very much he just had to murder these gals. In his mind they represented weakness and that's why he did it.

If ya are still with me, hang on to your seat because the way this city operates there are certain laws which control what can or cannot take place. For instance, nothin' can happen to anyone down there without the fact that they've agreed to it; even the stuff which makes a person feel sick to think about. That's right and, no, I've not lost my mind. These women agreed to be murdered by Ben in the way that they did because it made sense in their lives and fit into a place with their greater needs, like a jigsaw.

I'm talkin' subtlety here; vast kinds of laws which cause events and suchlike to come and go in a mysterious way. Obviously, it ain't so simple as these ladies wakin' up one morning and decidin' that rather than goin' off to work, they would just wander around until someone like Ben came along to murder 'em because they didn't like their jobs anymore. Hell no, there's more to this business of livin' in the City than meets the eye.

You folks always get what you need and what you need may not always seem the same as what you want but, trust me, it is.

Take this one gal which Ben snuffed at the beginning of his rampage; let's call her Abbey.

Abbey had it all: a good career, looks, brains and money comin' out'a her ears. She also had cancer. It was in the early stages; so early that no doctor no matter how good he was could have detected it. But you folks got your own built-in devices; sensors which keep an eye on stuff like that and Abbey knew, somewhere deep inside, that she had this terrible thing growin' in her guts and that, in the long run, she'd lose everything - includin' her good looks.

Well, she'd known enough people who'd gone through all the treatments. No hair, thin, weak. If that was the cure, she'd rather die. This was the essence of her plan, more or less, but how it works is complicated and I don't even know if it'd help for me to explain. Suffice it to say that you're all a helluva lot smarter than you think and already Abbey was lookin' for a way out. Enter Ben.

Through a string of carefully designed actions, which you might call coincidence, Abbey found herself down the wrong street at the wrong time, on her own, and part of her was lookin' for Ben just like Ben was lookin' for her. He strangled Abbey, sat her upright in one of those covered bus stops, and went home feelin' better than ever. Her money and other belongings were intact, just like her figure and good looks. Maybe ya get the picture just a little better when ya look at it like that.

This is how things work: nothin' happens that somebody don't say *okay*. Ben and Abbey were just helpin' each other and Ben would have carried on night after friggin' night except that his own secret self was gettin' pissed off in the extreme and eventually he had to admit that this cure of his was simply not workin'. He hated himself probably even more than before, if the truth be known, and this is the real reason why he finally slipped up. Ben would never have been caught, no way no how, if that wasn't what he'd decided he needed.

It's one helluva strong magnet; need. Ya use it

every day in lots'a different ways; lookin' for a spouse,

or a new job, or even a case of the *trots*. Ben needed to

kill. He needed to get rid of the weakness inside

himself. Whether you like it or not, he was well in my

vision and I had my spotlights on him, full power, the

entire time.

Now, I ain't sayin' I made him kill these gals, no

way, but he couldn't have killed 'em unless it worked

for them all.

What's that? Ya think he was just an evil

bastard? I can't blame ya, I guess, but ya gotta forget

about good and evil or right and wrong for just a

minute. Ya talk about forgiveness and ya read about it

in books but what if forgiveness had less to do with the things themselves than it had to do with acceptance?

What if it turned out that this city is so perfect in its imperfections that no one can really die and nobody can ever truly fail? If all those folks who keep pushin' and shovin' to get to the top or to get one over on the other guy just stopped for one friggin' minute and thought about it, they'd maybe realize that there ain't no way to get to the top and that it ain't gonna' make any difference anyways because you're all just about as Goddamned perfect as you're gonna' get. If ya really knew that and stopped hatin' yourselves so much for not bein' good enough then there'd be no place for people like Ben because there wouldn't be anybody wantin' to die in that sort of way.

This is the bare bones of it and I know it ain't easy to understand because it don't seem fair. I know it don't and I know that some of ya's have had things like this happen in your lives and maybe lost somebody ya loved, so I won't talk about it anymore if that's what ya want. Anyway, I s'pose you are still wantin' to know how Ben was finally caught? Okay, but just one more thing about right and wrong and good and evil; so bear with me.

The way this city was made, in the beginnin' when it was fresh and everyone knew that they'd live forever, it was also understood that there was no point in takin' another life for any reason whatsoever.

Because of the fact that ya all knew this, ya also knew

it wouldn't make any difference to the person who

died, but it would to you; and let's face it, ya gotta'nuff

to worry about keepin' your own selves straight

without havin' to make amends to some dead guy

who's only gonna come back and have another chance

anyway. Well, enough of that. That was then and this

is now and, in time, alotta ya just forgot about the way

the City really works and started thinkin' about good

verses evil. Then, some of ya decided that you needed

someone to actually BE THAT EVIL so ya could see

how the new concept worked. This was your own

original idea and ya should'a realized that ya can't

have the good guys without someone else bein' the bad. Remember, ya get what ya need and that's what you did.

Anyway, the good guys finally caught up with ol' Ben. He'd already given up on himself and it was only then that I lost sight of him and he wandered out'a the light. It was just after he'd murdered his seventeenth victim. The night was cold and the sky was pouring down with stabbin' icy raindrops. Instead of runnin' away or hidin' the body, he just sat down on a park bench and cried. She was layin' with her head on his lap when they found him early in the morning and he'd been cryin because it had finally sunk home that after seventeen killings he still hated himself and still felt weak inside. In fact, he felt even weaker and if that was the case then probably there just wasn't any strength in him at all, so he knew there was no point in tryin' anymore. Ya see, he stopped believing in himself and just gave up. Somebody else might have handled all these bad feelings a helluva lot differently. Think about some of them do-gooders that you know. The folks who go out at night and give soup or blankets to the down-and-outs who live on the street. They ain't always doin' it because they have a great self image. Hell no, alotta them are so full of self doubt and feel so worthless that they try to give their lives value by helpin' others. Hey, don't get me wrong, it's a good thing and somebody's gotta do it but I'm just tryin' to show ya that Ben maybe could'a gone that way with his feelings - just the same way those do-gooders might become like him. Anyway, the police found him, all scrunched up and cold and they took him away.

Ben made all the headlines and that helped his self image but not by much. The jury found him guilty which he was but at least he finally got some help. I catch a glimpse of him now and then, movin' nearer. I was never too worried about him; like I don't worry about the rest of ya. I kept a light on, so to speak, but he had to find his own way. Ya see, no one can ever get really lost, just a little waylaid if they make a wrong turn like Ben did.

CHAPTER 4

Love Me Tender

The King is dead. Long live the King.

Myself, I don't like rock and roll much. Give me a tango or a polonaise any day of the week. Still, I gotta hand it to him, he made a great big noise while he had the chance and split while the goin' was good. So, any of ya's who are still tryin' to keep your hero alive by tellin' yourselves that he's been washin' his socks at the local laundromat or baggin' groceries at the local QuickyMart had better accept that he's here, with me, and still shakin' those hips.

There's still a lotta sortin' out to do. Let's face it, it can't be easy livin' such a high flyin' kinda life for so many years, only to come here and find that the gold jumpsuits and mile-long limos weren't what it was all about. Anyway, I've got him nicely settled now on the 67th Floor, doin' office work mostly. Heck, there's a whole bunch of 'em livin' together: Buddy, Janis, Jimmy, Keith, even Norma Jean spent some time there sortin' things out and building from her tragedy. I'll tell ya one thing, Elvis would be the first to admit that not anyone would have given him a second look if he'd stayed around and just plain grew old. So, like I was sayin,' he split.

Lots of you folks are still findin' it hard to let go of him. Hell, the mailbag alone is enough to make the old head spin. He gets mail from little kids who weren't even born when he died, but I s'pose as long as you folks need legends, Elvis will be King.

I remember when he first arrived, what a bunch of commotion. Not only did he call himself the *King* but he said he was from *Graceland*. Okay, I thought, have it your way. I mean he had figured out one thing for himself and there was just no way he was gonna hang around down there with all you folks while he got old and you forgot him. You know it and I know it.

Elvis was like all the brightest stars in the sky. If they stay up there, night after night, we kinda get used to 'em and eventually they fade away. Now the ones that suddenly flare up and shoot across the heavens like the Fourth of July capture our imagination and admiration. I gotta give him one thing, he sure had style.

Ya know, there's a lotta musicians and show-biz folks who go AWOL and cut out early. It's this fear of failure that haunts so many of you folks and gets ya screwed up inside. I guess it's a type of hunger and maybe a need to be loved, who knows. Take Elvis, for instance, he tried to pretend that his comin' here was some kind of accident. Now, we all know that just ain't true and I try to get him to talk about things; you know, the stuff that frightened him and maybe still does. It just ain't as cut and dried as you think. You keep all of your memories when ya come here and all of the feelings, good and bad, that go with 'em. I don't really need Elvis to talk about his life, I already know it, but it would help him let go of the past and he could move on.

There I go again, it's the same old stuff ain't it? This business of goin' with your true feelings and lettin' yourselves be guided by this here beacon that separates those who want to move forward and those who don't.

Elvis stayed a boy all his life and, growin' up, he was one of the brightest kids you ever wanna meet. Poor guy, he had more energy than he knew what to do with and I had all I could do not to cheer him on or give him a little extra help; which ya know would not have been strictly fair to the rest of ya. Again, I keep tellin' ya, I don't worry about folks the way you do down there and I was definitely never too worried about him. So long as he could keep makin' music and gettin' that love from his fans, he was happy but he just never gotta 'round to learning about lovin' back. He will, you'll see. Like folks say, there's one thing we got plenty of here and that's time. Ya can't rush folks, they gotta deal with stuff when they're good and ready.

What's that? Why didn't he just retire and spend the rest of his life enjoyin' all of that do-re-me? That's a fair question, I s'pose but if ya'd been listenin' ya'd know that money had nothin' to do with it. Adoration and love; that was the Big E's game. Ya see, it's all about choices and needs and if it sounds like I am goin' around in circles here, well maybe I am but ya gotta understand how much your needs can affect your own lives and quit blamin' everyone else.

Anyway, Elvis needed to be loved and adored. He had the hungriest ego you'd ever seen and deep down, underneath all of that shakin' and shoutin' he was afraid. Nobody wants to get old and find that the people who are s'pose to love 'em have just cast 'em aside all forgotten.

Now, like a lotta stuff that happens in the City, his death prob'ly seemed like an accident. Well, there ain't no such thing, it just looks that way. I mean, ya wouldn't really have a very good week if ya woke up one morning and realized that on Saturday ya were gonna choke to death on a chicken sandwich. These things happen on sort of a secret level and ya design your life in such a smooth and even way that ya hardly ever notice what a good job you're doin'. That's about the only real law there is in the City and it was made this way so I wouldn't need to be doin' everything for ya. How the hell am I s'posed to know what ya really want or what ya really need? Sure as, you know what, if it was left to me I'd get it wrong sooner or later. You folks are like the man who has everything and when it comes time to buy him a gift, it's either gonna be right or very very wrong. That's where those free will powers come in to play and your own magical gifts as creators. Like I keep tellin' ya; what ya need and concentrate on, ya get. It's a simple as that.

Listen to that little voice in the back of your head and try to follow what it's sayin'. That's the only sure way you're ever gonna' make sense of anything. I mean, if ya had a kid who wasn't even smart enough to figure one thing out for themselves or who was so friggin' dull that he had zero interests or plans for his life, ya wouldn't just keep doin' everything for them, would ya? Hell no. Ya'd throw 'em out on their ass and let 'em figure it out for themselves. Now, just because this kid of yours got it wrong now and again, or went the long way about doin' things, ya wouldn't step in and make it all easy for him; not if ya really cared about him ya wouldn't. No, you'd keep an eye on him because you've done your best when he was growin' up and tried to give him all of the sense and mental agility ya could, so he wouldn't need to be callin' ya on the pocket phone all the time askin' what he should or should not do. If ya's done your job right as a parent then ya'd know that your kids are gonna get there, sooner or later. Like some folks say, kids grow up despite their parents and if ya think about that ya'd all realize that it makes sense.

Painful? Sure, it's sometimes painful to watch, I ain't gonna lie. The hardest thing about lovin' someone is givin' them the space to be themselves. I mean, I'm sittin' here keepin' this old lighthouse burnin' bright and I can see some poor bastard goin' hell bent for election right toward disaster. Can I do somethin' about it? Not really, that wouldn't be fair and it sure as hell would not help him neither. Lessons are out there wherever ya go. Sometimes they are disguised as other people and other times they might come at ya as a tragedy but they are all challenges that you've taken on to help ya learn.

Just remember what I been sayin' — ya get what ya need and if ya keep remindin' yourself that, above everything else, ya need to be happy then maybe most of your troubles would be small and more of your time could be spent smilin'. What d'ya think? Make any sense to ya? It should 'cause there ain't no way I'm gonna lie.

CHAPTER 5

In The Beginning …

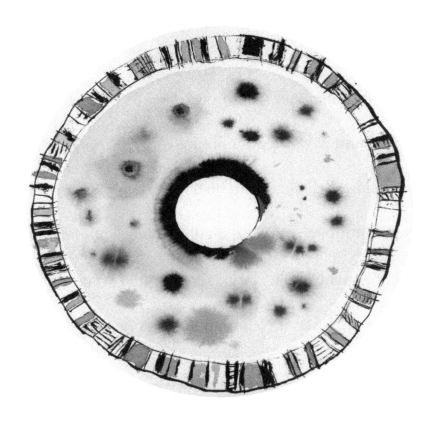

What, exactly, is the truth? That's what you're thinkin' isn't it. Well, the truth is ... I don't really know what the truth is ... I just know that I can't lie to ya.

This City's so much a part of me that it's like I automatically am just me and ... well ... everything kinda takes care of itself but within my view, so to speak. Like the way your body takes care of itself without you even having to think about it, and I guess I'm sorta like that, just doin' what I've always done. And ya know what? I can't remember a time when I wasn't lookin' after things from way up here, just like I'm doin' now.

Don't get me wrong, I'm not perpetual or anything like that and, just between us two, there was a time when there was nobody else ... just me. True, I swear to ya, way back when, and I mean way back, it was just me and my thoughts. Now, this ain't gonna be so easy to explain to someone from the City so don't be shy about askin' questions if ya ain't followin' or if I sound like I've flipped my lid. Okay? Good. That's the way.

Let's see, how does that go again? *In the beginning there was the word and the word was made flesh.* If that sounds familiar it should and I don't apologize for usin' it 'cause that sums things up pretty good.

Ya see, long ago when I was here alone, with just my thoughts and dreams, everything kinda happened inside my mind and the dreams and the pictures just came and went. Some things maybe held my attention a bit longer than others but, on the whole, stuff was just comin' alive inside of me and, the way I see it now, it was like I was exercising — buildin' my muscles so that I'd be able to create this here city in one almighty explosion of three-dimensional glory. That's what I think anyway and maybe ya got your own ideas and I'd like to hear 'em sometime if ya do.

So, to give ya an idea of what it was like, most of my time was spent just bein' and playin' with my own infinite talents. And, before ya ask, I haven't a friggin' clue where I came from or when and maybe that's why I'm so useless with clocks and things like that, I don't know. I can't feel time passin' the same way you do but I move around between years and weeks and days and minutes and centuries the same way you walk from your living room to your kitchen. I'll tell ya this for free, time and space is putty in my hands. Ya might say it's my stock and trade.

Now, for you guys in the City, ya only really have to worry about today then the day after and the day after that, etcetera. I still gotta keep an eye on everyone who ever was or will be livin' in that city but it's a whole different ball game so I won't even attempt to explain 'cause I'm not so sure myself. What I can tell ya is that because of the oddball laws of the City, I gotta make sure that this here lighthouse of mine is flexible enough to keep an eye on every single one of ya no matter when or where you're livin' your lives so that things keep runnin' smoothly for everyone.

Think about it like this. You all can remember stuff that happened maybe twenty or thirty years ago but ya don't have any recollection of the things that haven't happened yet; how could ya, right? But for me, well I'm rememberin' and reactin' to stuff that has happened, might have happened, could possibly happen — plus all the infinite permutations of the aforementioned — and that's a whole lotta rememberin'. Keep in mind, too, that it's all just as real as the stuff you get up to in the City. There's people who haven't been born yet who are dreamin' dreams — big dreams — and those are the kinda things I gotta help make happen when the time comes, ya understand? Maybe a little, right? Hey, don't worry, I'm lookin' after you and that's the main thing ya should be focused on.

So, goin' back a bit, as I was sayin', here I was with all of this stuff inside of me and it was like this world with ideas that were growin' stronger and not going to just disappear. Little by little these dreams made it clear that they wanted to express themselves in a way that just bein' inside of me couldn't do so I guess ya could say it was causin' me some considerable discomfort.

It was a hellishly painful time for me, I can tell ya, and it wasn't easy tryin' to decide how to make things right. I wondered if maybe I'd been abusin' myself or somethin' because up until then, I had no concept of what being alone really meant. Then, with all of these dreams and ideas moving around inside of me, I began to feel very alone and it was then that I knew I had to either let my dreams have their separation from me or let them eat me alive, which would mean every thing disappearin' forever.

What did I do? Good question cause I nearly died, turnin' loose all of this beauty, and if I told ya I was frightened that would only be the half of it. At least down in the City ya got someone, like family or friends, but I had no one and it was only through pure guts and stubbornness that I got through it.

There's no easy way to explain what happened but if I asked ya to jump into a blazin' inferno at the bottom of some giant canyon and said, *Trust me, it will be fine.* What would ya do? Either ya would or ya wouldn't, am I right? Well, that's pretty much how it was for me and the outcome could only be one of two possibilities. Either I'd be done forever or my dreams, my children, my angels and my gods would have their own lives and freedom; instead of just a lot of possibly great stuff that was bottled up inside'a me.

So, bein' driven by what must have been the king of all migraine headaches, I jumped and ... well, the rest is history and that's basically why you're able to come and spend some time with me today. I can tell ya one thing, the noise and the agony that went along with all of this explosive release of ideas and energy was nearly too much. Whoever wrote, *In the beginning there was the word*, should've added that the word had four letters and echoed across the new universe like no sound ever had before and, bein' the First Sound, it had a volume that would split your head open and smash the insides into tiny pieces. But, you're gonna ask, did I feel better? I felt incredible!

Just focus that mind of yours for a minute on all the best things you've ever done. Ya know, the things that ya did a great job on, all by yourself with no help from nobody, and then magnify that a zillion times.

That might be about half as great as I felt *In The*

Beginning. Who'da known it was just gonna get better?

CHAPTER 6

Dinner At Eight

Hey, look at the time will ya. I been doin' all the talkin' while ya prob'ly got things to do and places to go. What's that, ya don't? Well if ya wanna give me a hand clearin' up some of this mess I can tell ya a little more about the city and what it's really like bein' up here keepin' a watchful eye on things.

Ya see, maybe ya think I get a lotta visitors. Prob'ly seems to you that everyone must be knockin' on that door and askin' all kinds of crazy questions but it just ain't so.

Who knows why, I'm sure I don't. I mean, what could be easier than gettin' it straight from the horse's mouth? There's no problem for me in ya's all askin'. Guess folks have gotten so friggin' used to just acceptin' all the crap they create for themselves then spendin' so much time feelin' like they are somehow victims that they ain't never thought to just stop and ask me some questions. I am tellin' ya this for free and it ain't somethin' everyone knows: alls ya gotta do is ask and believe that you will get the answers you need. Because sure as summer follows spring, you will. There ain't all that many real honest-to-goodness truths in this City but that's definitely one of them.

Yeh, yeh, yeh; I know, people do ask. They're askin' all the time and for all sorts of crazy shit. Ya know, new cars, money, stuff — magic, magic, magic. Listen here, the secret is in your imagination, which is one and the same thing. Whatever ya can picture in your mind and keep close to your heart, ya can have. Oh yea, and you'll usually get it fairly quickly — no waitin' — if it's what ya believe and what ya truly feel a need for. So, the secret is: Want, Need, Belief ... and a touch a Passion won't go amiss neither. Those things are the secret to more wondrous miracles than you might ever have time to dream about.

Of course ya don't think so; nobody does. How the hell can gettin' what ya need and what ya want be easy? Hell knows, the City is hard and life can be a bitch; I understand that. But I'll tell ya a few other things they believe down there and that's this bull that *Life has to be difficult or it don't count*, and another one that gets me is, *Don't dream too much or you'll just be disappointed*;

but the one that really makes me nuts is, *Don't trust anyone 'cause you'll only wind up gettin' hurt.*

Where d'ya get these ideas from? It sure as hell ain't from me and it sure as hell ain't the truth. Like I said before, truth's a very funny thing and just believin' in things like that can make 'em true enough to screw up your entire life. Now, remember I said that so ya can tell 'em, okay? If ya believe life's gonna be a load of crap, well then it will be and there ain't nothin' I nor anyone else can do about it until you're ready to open up and listen.

Anyway, I got sidetracked a bit there but people don't come to me for answers all that often. Maybe they're just scared or don't think about it, I'm not sure, but they just don't. It's like they'd rather take the long way around, if ya know what I mean. That's fine by me; no skin off my nose. A lotta the times they prefer pesterin' Jesus or one of the others and askin' them to play middle man and pass a message to me; like I don't already know what's goin' on anyhow? Funny it ain't but, hey, I don't mind. As far as I'm concerned ya don't get somethin' if ya don't ask and even if it seems like I don't always come through for ya, I can promise ya this for nothin' - I'd be happy ta give ya everything I have if I could but some of the times you're just askin' without believin'.

Let me put it another way. If ya ask for somethin'-a change or better days or whatever — and then ya turn around and doubt the value of your own self, I can't do much to help. It's like puttin' up a wall between the two of us and too much of the time you're only askin' me 'cause ya don't have enough faith in yourselves to make it happen naturally. Like I keep sayin' over and over again, if ya don't believe in your own power ya can't believe in me and you won't get diddly.

Just relax, take a deep breath and let it flow. Hey, things can't get any worse unless you want 'em to.

Right, enough about me, let's talk about you. I ain't even had the good manners to ask what ya came here for have I. Don't worry, I will when I got five minutes but let me make it up to ya. I mean, ya said you weren't in any big hurry so if ya still got some time why not kick back and stay for dinner? I got some people comin' 'round in about an hour or somethin' like that. Tell ya what, split the difference and call it eight o'clock; remember I told ya that I'm not so good with clocks. Anyhow, hang around and you'll get answers to your questions and prob'ly some other stuff ya hadn't bargained for.

Ya see, there's the bell already. Go ahead, answer it. If I know anything about anything, it's Buddha. He's always early and always hungry.

I gotta turn something off in the kitchen; you let him in and then maybe take a seat on that big sofa over there … just 'til they get used to ya. Most of my friends ain't accustomed ta havin' folks from the City

just pop in ya see, so sit back and play it cool; ya don't

wanna spook 'em.

Buddha, what a surprise! I guessed ya'd be the first one.

Here, have a beer and take a seat.

Ya see, he likes his drink and his food and he

loves ta socialize. Sit down, relax and I'll let the others

in. You just sit, relax and pay close attention or you're

gonna miss somethin'.

Okay, I think that went pretty good. Ya enjoyed

yourself didn't ya? Did ya learn anything? I tell ya, the

look on your face when Buddha kicked off his sandals

and put his feet up on your lap. Priceless! Ya didn't

know what the hell to do but you did good by massagin' 'em.

So what do ya think of 'em all? What d'ya mean, you don't remember? Nothing at all? Oh, then ya do remember rubbin' his feet, but that's it? It's okay I guess; that's what comes from livin' in the City. Ya can't keep your mind focused on stuff that ain't made out'a concrete and glass. Don't worry, I understand. Ya enjoyed yourself, I think; it looked like it.

So, let me tell ya about it and promise to stop me if I go too fast.

Okay, so eight o'clock rolls 'round and ya'd already been talkin' with Early-bird-Buddha for some while. Ya both had moved on to the whisky by the time the others arrived so ya weren't feelin' any pain, not from what I could see. Buddha, he couldn't even stand, or maybe he just didn't want to, 'cause he just sat there when the others arrived. It was funny. Ya both just smiled and waved to Isis and Osiris. Jesus, Mohammed, Zeus and Shiva were all very polite, as usual, and pretended not to notice how ... well ... relaxed you both were. Hey, don't look at me like that. Ya didn't embarrass yourself and, besides, they made up for it during dinner.

Well, there we all were, sittin' round the table, enjoyin' ourselves. There were ten of us, includin' you two, which is an important fact, so don't forget.

Okay, I says. *We gotta fairly important guest tonight. Ya all know how rare it is for me to get visitors from the City, so relax and just be yourselves. But try to remember who you are.*

Well, things were goin' better than I expected and nobody started makin' trouble for anyone else or tryin' to goad anyone into an argument. Ya know what they say about avoiding religion and politics in mixed company? Well, there's prob'ly some truth in that where you come from but up here, it wouldn't be any fun if we didn't. So, the old Ambrosia was flowin' free and things began to loosen up nicely until you, of all people, kicked open a hornet's nest. And I don't mean just a few little sting-ass hornets; I'm talkin' big, nasty, kick-boxin' suckers.

So, are ya ready for this? Just as innocent and wide-eyed as ya please, ya turn to Jesus and, lookin' him right in the eye, you ask, *What about original sin, then? Is that why ya let those Romans nail ya to the cross?*

Well, that was all the rest of 'em needed. Shiva joins in with his or her scented, innocent voice. *Yes, dear Jesus, what about original sin? Do explain it to us. We'd love to hear all about it.*

Or any sin for that matter. Old Zeus just had to get his two cents worth in and he smiles at ya as he says it. But don't look so worried. JC handled it beautifully. He hardly batted an eyelid and just sat for a minute or two, lookin' around the room, before he settled his eyes on you and answered, as cool as a cucumber.

Well, now that you ask, and he takes time choosin' his words so that leaves the rest of us hangin', *I didn't come up with the Original Sin idea and definitely not in the way our special guest means it. The rest of you should know better but if that's the way you want to play then don't blame me if you get more than you bargained for.*

Hey, I wish ya could remember. JC was in great form and I think maybe he even enjoyed it. I mean, who really gives him the chance to spout off anymore, like in the ol' days? Anyway, listen to this next bit, ya might learn somethin'

I was speaking to a lack of knowledge; like an empty vessel that needs to be filled with the things that really matter. It is sinful, in a way, if you spend your days and years not doing much of anything and don't even try to fill up that emptiness —

that potential — with things of value. And, if we're talkin'

about being sinful, you're committing the most unforgivable sins

against yourselves if you don't follow your heart and go for the

things that benefit you in a true and fulfilling way. Of course,

what that might be is going to be different for everyone and

sometimes you tend to brush the truth away and just consider it

as daydreaming. What you're really doing is just continuing to

fumble in the dark, being miserable and unhappy. So, I suppose

you can call that type of behavior a sin, if you feel happier

thinking like that. But if you accept this ridiculous idea of sin, it

means you must also accept that you're not perfect and you are

somehow flawed, which probably means that inside, deep inside,

you don't really feel you're worth much. That's a shame, don't ya

think, and if it was me living down there in that wonderful City

I'd go for it all and do everything I could to follow my instincts and, even if I didn't get everything right, I'd sure have one

helluva good time trying!

Ya should'a seen the expression on your face.

Jesus has this way of lookin' inside a person and given'

them an answer that really shakes 'em up, deep down,

where it counts — which I think is what he did to you.

So, he just smiles, pauses for a bit, and continues.

The word I used, which has been so very misused ever

since, actually means emptiness and lack, which in itself implies

potential. If you are lacking in something, it always means that

the possibility or potential is there, hidden, but waiting for you to

fulfill any lack by making improvements. Sin is what happens

when you let yourself down or ignore your potential, that's all.

Holy cow! I can't help it if folks want to distort everything I ever said and change my meaning to suit their own politics now, can I.

If I tell you that you have sinned then I tell you that you have let yourself down; no one else. Of course, the good thing about sin, as a concept, is that you have as many lifetimes as you need to sort yourself out and even when you get things wrong, you can grow from those mistakes.

And, one other thing, you will not ever go to heaven because there just isn't one. The only hell you'll ever know is the one you create for yourself and you create that by choosing the roads that bring misery and unhappiness. Now, does that answer your question?

I'm thinkin' by this time your head must have been really spinnin'. Not only were ya confused by the rapid-fire delivery of JC's comments but Shiva was changin' shapes and sexes faster than you could follow. Does it matter what sex? I mean, spirit has no sex but, just the same, Shiva is the sexiest of them all. HeSheThemMe - it's all the same; genderbender city - ya know what I mean? It's all about *the skin* in your world. Here, in The Lighthouse, we have no skin … in the game, or otherwise. So as I was sayin', you were next to Shiva who had just morphed from a bearded god to a powerful female; her yin to your yang. Well, what happened next … it was somethin' else. Ya see, without much of a warning, she started to put the moves on ya and was had her arms all over you; so much so that she began to wrap herself around you like a snake. Truth is, and you probably don't remember, she had actually turned into one.

Sssay, have you ever wondered what really happened in the garden at Eden? she asked, her tongue flickin' in and outta your ear. *Would you like to know the real reason that Adam and Eve were keeping company with that serpent?*

Ya sorta gulped and managed to gently push Shiva away who, thankfully, resumed a more female form - but with so many arms she was more in control than she had been as a snake; so think yourself lucky she didn't wrap you up and take you away to some eternal ashram in the celestial netherworld . Anyway, as I was sayin' or, rather, as Shiva was sayin'.

Why, that was me of course, you sweet thing. Who else has such cunning and can be so clever? The City has done a good job in changing the truth about my involvement in that, too, just like they do with most things. I wasn't up to no good, Honey Chile, why no indeed. I was only trying to help those two by planting a few seeds of a hunger for knowledge and truth-almighty. Hallelujah!

Why, honey, it's only those contortions in history that messed the whole thing up for me: CREATION. Getting tossed out of that garden. Hell, the entire thing was an illusion anyway and I chose the serpent because she represented energy and your basic instincts. Why if you just look at a snake sometimes, when it's all curled up a'sleepin', then you look at it again when it's all agitated and hungry; Lord, all that power and might just waitin' there with only one thing on its mind — to get fed and to grow!

Hell, it's only instinct and if you all would take advantage of

your own strength and fertility you'd all find yourselves growin' in

the most wonderful of ways. Amen and hallelujah!

Now, Shiva, we all know that you chose to take the form

of that snake because you were hoping to frighten that poor couple

and take one or both of them for yourself. Jehovah piped up.

You know it as well as we do. Then he turned to you and

sorta whispered as if he wanted you to side with him.

You see, back in those days us gods had more to do with the City

and that might be because it was still fairly new and there

weren't so many of you hustling about as there is nowadays. I

guess you wanted us nearby until you found your feet and, yes, it's

true that some of the children born back then were mixed-

blessings; you know, half-human and half-gods. Anyway, who the

hell's interested in why Shiva transformed into a serpent? It's all ancient history; water under the bridge, and it didn't work out the way she hoped anyhoo!

Now, I think what we would really like to know is how you all managed to make such a damned mess of things? I mean, everything we taught you has just been turned around, distorted and blown out of proportion. It's that City ... it's just gotten too big! Jehovah chimed in then sat back and went silent.

There's somethin' kinda depressing about Jehovah. Don't get me wrong, he's great at carin' and lovin' and tryin' to help but he just turns too damned serious for my tastes ... just can't seem to lighten up and have some fun. Ya know what I mean?

Well, ya sat lookin' at Jehovah for the longest time and I think it was just beginnin' to sink in that you were sharin' dinner with honest ta goodness gods.

CHAPTER 7

Holy Moses and The Theory of Relativity

I know this has been a strange day for ya and, all things considered, you handled it pretty well. Phew, if it was me, I'd have been climbin' those walls lookin' for a way out, but fast. You, well you're different. Ya gotta sense of openness that most of you City folks seem to have lost or forgotten about. So, all that bein' said, you were starin' at Jehovah for what seemed an eternity and I think we were all feelin' a bit sorry for ya, I mean the pressure must have been intense. Then you slowly reached over and helped yourself to a big swig of the ol' Ambrosia before you replied.

I don't think you're being fair, ya said, as honest as anything. *It's not just us down there who've messed things up and besides, the way I understand the City is that is isn't screwed* up so much after all. It might be a bit constipated and confused now and then but we're all learning and you gotta have some faith that we'll get there. And, if you're so bothered about it, why not give us another chance and try being more honest about your reasons for helping? I don't think you ever were really that interested in helping us. Some of you aren't much better than Elvis or the rest of them up on the 67th floor. I think you probably did it for attention and fame. I mean, it's true that some of the things you've said and did made an impact but if we've distorted everything, like you say, just to make it suit our own selfishness then maybe it's because you weren't very clear. Maybe you just didn't do a very good job! The City's a hard enough place to live in without us having to turn all of your 'wisdom' inside out trying to understand it.

We were all surprised at your balls, I gotta say and if that wasn't enough, you reached over and tapped Jesus on the shoulder, interrupting his conversation with Mohammed; and between the two of us, you were right to think he hadn't been paying much attention.

How hard would it have been to just spit it out, in black and white, and tell us exactly what the score was? Would it have been some kind of sin to simply explain what we should do and what we should aim for to achieve happiness? Jesus Christ, you don't have the first idea of how busy and under pressure we all get just trying to manage day by day without having to unravel ancient mysteries or become mystics. It wouldn't have hurt you to just keep it simple, like mathematics. I mean, no matter how many times I add up two plus two it is always going to equal four.

I enjoyed that moment, I can tell ya. Jesus was nearly speechless and he was just about to shape his thin lips into some kind of response when Moses pulled up a chair and joined in.

Hope you'll forgive my intrusion, he said, all pompous and stuffy like, *but I was in the neighborhood and couldn't help being drawn here by that debate of yours.* He took your hand and smiled. *As for you, my friend, you were indeed given laws and they couldn't have been any clearer than they were; straight from the source. How could they? After all, the big guy there gave you words, carved in stone, one letter at a time. It was basically given to you on a platter, or on tablets in this case, but you still managed to mess things up.*

Good ol' patient Moses The only time I've ever known him lose his temper was over those damned tablets ... those friggin' commandments.

Ya prob'ly've heard the story before but I'll tell ya anyway. Here I was, keepin' Moses and all them Israelites in my view. The lighthouse was workin' overtime, ya might say, and the beacon was really bein' pushed to its limit. There was a lotta trouble all around the City at that time but I especially had to keep my eye on Moses and make sure I could give him all the help he needed. I tell ya, it was a beautiful sight, all of 'em walkin' proud and strong in the light of the beacon waitin' to finally be led out'a Egypt.

Moses had begged me to let him go down and help. The poor bastard was even mistaken for Jesus at one point and it took all the tricks I knew to save his skin and to keep him from cashin' his chips in early. Anyway he wasn't makin' much headway with the Jews and it was obvious that we'd have to come up with somethin' amazing if we wanted to keep them in the light and ensure they'd stay that way long after he left.

It just wasn't enough, I guess, that they all wanted to flee Egypt and get away from Pharaoh. They had to really feel a deep powerful need for a new life, just like I'd promised them so many years before. I owed it to them and had to give 'em something solid to build their lives around. It was like everything I'd promised was a tree and they'd be the vines, clingin' to it and growin' stronger toward the light.

Well, like any good leader would do, I gave Moses an outline; a set of twelve commandments for the Jews to use and as a reminder of how things really were.

Now, this was by no means an easy task. Moses and I argued for days over the words and what should or should not be included. Hell, we even argued about what it should be written on. To tell ya the truth, I'da been fine with a few sheets of papyrus but Moses was sure they'd only get lost or thrown out by mistake. So, we finally agreed that some stone slabs would do the trick and I'll be damned if those didn't get lost anyhow.

Well, once they were lost, the editing and changes started creepin' in and I can't point the finger at anyone in particular. After all, nobody's got a perfect memory and when you're passing stuff down through the years there's gonna be a certain amount of embroidery that takes place. What really got me was that two of the most important ones were just taken out, just like that, so I'll share them with you now, right here.

Above everything, believe in yourself and in God's love. Think about it and you'll understand just how important that is. If ya get that right, most other stuff will fall into place. Then there was the other one:

Be true to yourself and to others through these many lifetimes. Well, okay, maybe it's a bit 'out there' but I wanted to let 'em know their actions have consequences for all eternity. Those weren't the exact words, and you might be right, maybe it was too much.

And while I'm on the subject, neither me nor Moses ever once said, Thou shalt not commit adultery. That one just crept in because you all seem to have this problem with jealousy; that's a real stinker. Why you all feel ya need to own somethin' even another person is beyond me. And while I'm on the subject of jealousy and being misquoted, the coveting another man's wife is another bizarre rewrite of what was originally a warning against coveting another person's life in any way. It really makes me angry sometimes and I should'a learned by then that puttin' somethin' in writing doesn't guarantee it won't be messed with.

Well, anyway, Moses did a damned good job and it was hard work. Hell, by the time he was finished, he looked like he'd aged fifty years and what does the poor bastard find when he hauls them tablets back to his people? They're havin' a House Party and dancin 'round a golden calf. Mad? He was furious, who wouldn't be. Never mind, it's like most problems; they all work out in the end. But those Israelites, they always were suspicious of Moses; even of me for that matter; always wantin' everything in writing, which I s'pose ya can't blame 'em. They had more than their share of bad times and plenty of folks took advantage of them or lied to 'em before Moses came along. So, to make things better, a new beginning if you will, I made a covenant and that seemed to help. Believe me, even today, it would stand in any court and that's sayin' plenty! Too bad they didn't keep it safe, but that's life in the City.

What's that? Oh, sorry, you wanted to know what Moses had to say. He said plenty and so did you but at least you had the ears to listen with, too.

There's only one law and it couldn't be simpler. Whatever you think on with enough power will be made real in your life.

The problem is that sometimes fear can transform a bad thing into a desire just because your mind is so busy worrying that, before you know it, the very thing you fear has come to pass.

Good or bad, you make these things happen and you make them

real. I'm sorry, but that's just how it is and the sooner you City

folks get to grips with that concept the sooner you can all start

spreading your wings again and do some fancy flying.

Yeh, I think you were happy with his answer. I'm

not sure it made sense to ya but at least you spent some

time thinkin' it over until another guest sat himself

down right across from ya; right between Isis and

Osiris. It was Albert Einstein and while not in the same

league god-wise, he has one helluva head for the

creativity stakes. Of course, he was his usual sloppy

self with that baggy sweater, crumpled trousers and

floppy shoes but ya can get away with that look when

you're him.

You should not be encouraging these people to be creative, he said, naturally soundin' smarter than everyone else which he maybe is. *Just because everyone can create that doesn't mean we should encourage it.*

I really hate it when he says, WE, which he says all the time.

I mean, just look at the state of things. Most of your creations down there are more than inferior. In fact, many are absolutely diabolical!

Oh, and I suppose giving them the secret to life itself was using that big head of yours in a creative and useful way? Isis never liked Al but she was makin' a fair point I thought, but never would have said so.

What would you know about it, old woman? When I decided to share a way to help transform life in the City by taking on all of the crap that comes with being flesh and blood, I had no idea that the greater the gift, the greater would be their talent for exploiting it.

Moses tried to comfort him. *You should never have gone down there in the first place. If you would only have spoken to me first I could have told you that of all the people you might touch with your gift, only a select few will truly understand and take it upon themselves to use it wisely.*

Gott im Himmel! Why did I let myself fall down so with such foolish generosity? He poured himself a drink and topped up yours. *You see, my innocent friend, every now and then there are those, like myself and Moses here, who, knowing full well what it could mean, choose to take up residency in the City while retaining all of the knowledge and insights that most agree to leave behind. This is not easy but, just the same, there are a few brave souls who wish to serve and bring a greater understanding. Perhaps it was foolish and, as I learned, it proved to be as disastrous as giving gunpowder and a rifle to a Neanderthal.*

Still, because we love the City so much, we try. It is important that every now and then the minds of those in the City take a quantum leap into the vast sea of possibilities so they might move forward and advance their understanding. Sadly, for myself and others, the ones who possess the greatest power are often those with the greatest ignorance and fear. In fact, they fear everything and, most of all, they fear you and others like you.

Kindness is not everything, my friend, but it is disarming and a powerful weapon nonetheless. Those who understand this may have the least to lose so are often the most feared by those in power.

I could go on and on ad infinitum explaining myself and expressing regret but it would not change a thing. There were many who warned me of the danger that can come with great knowledge given to those who may not be ready. They also warned of the trouble I could bring to myself if I was unable to keep my true nature a secret. No matter! There will always be those who go ahead, moving forward, unfettered by the transformation of light into a world of relative darkness. They go, knowing they may be misunderstood or mistreated, and you have been dining with some of us tonight. There are many others who were unable to attend because they have already gone on to pursue other interests in alternative lighthouses well beyond this one.

Leonardo, my dearest friend, was greatly ridiculed and it is true that he badly mistimed his arrival. The materials and technology he needed had not yet advanced enough to do justice to his marvelous creations so, sadly, he could never have had enough time to deliver the potential of his thoughts. But it was not a waste and I have often told him so. Others have timed their arrival with greater success and were able to make use of his ideas and concepts, inspired by his purity of vision. There are things in this city that you know now which only exist because he planted the seeds in that past which you call time.

Ah yes, Time. I ripped it open for you and revealed reality in a way that was intended to open your eyes not blind your children. I sometimes feel I wasted a great truth but am pleased that, through this pain and devastation, the Lighthouse has continued to protect and guide those few who have begun to push for a more peaceful use of such great power. I do not feel such alarm or worry these days and believe that a greater

understanding will prevail.

My work, which is often misunderstood, is a truth. It is

the cornerstone of the Lighthouse and the city beneath. You build

your thoughts, brick upon brick, through eternity then sail swiftly

through time, unencumbered by space, and meet them as the fruit

of a tomorrow which is breathing life back into your 'now'.

I want only to share with you who you really are and

how much more you can be. How was I to know that you would

need to open these tiny flecks of life to peer inside? You cracked

open the essence of time and matter which came close to making

any form of tomorrow an impossibility. Please remember what I

share with you now and take it back with you.

Well you nodded at Al and gave him a look of

deep admiration with maybe even a little affection. He

thanked you for being so open. The conversation had gotten deep, I don't disagree, and I think Al sorta felt like a party pooper, which maybe he was. But then Mohammed had to go and get him really depressed.

Oh please, Mr Albert Einstein. Is it not the most very plain truth that, as in all things, you must have known beforehand what these ideas might bring? It must be even more so for you as you were working with the essence of Time itself. I cannot believe that your eyes could not see what your mind was doing!

Okay, Mohammed is known for his earthy approach. He don't pull punches and hasn't got much sympathy for those who behave like fools.

You're right. I admit it. Al picked up his hat and battered leather case and walked toward the door. *My greatest wish was to help and I had hoped that maybe one of you would have actually followed me down there. That maybe you would have used your special gifts to make certain our friends in the City would have the support and guidance they needed.* Poor Al ... he was so upset, he didn't bother to open the door; just walked right through it ... every single molecule of him. So, it was a bit of a sour note and the party quieted down for a bit, until Osiris and Zeus ganged up on Mohammed and blamed him for spoilin' the evening and hurtin' Einstein's feelings. He, in turn, blamed Moses for bringin' Al along and Moses blamed Isis for startin' the entire thing in the first place then she blamed Jehovah for bein' such a negative bastard because she probably felt guilty so couldn't think of anything better to say.

That's when you and me took our drinks across to that enormous plate-glass window over there and I got ya workin' with the spot-lights and magnifiers and radio equipment. In fact, I was lucky enough to spot a guy who was in need of some real illumination and extra-intensive care; and you were lucky enough to be here to help.

CHAPTER 8

Poor Tired John

Just south of the City, where the steel bridge crosses the river, we spy John - poor tired John. For countless years he'd played the part of daily slogger who took buses and subway trains every day to a job that was almost mind destroying. Every day he willingly shackled himself to a desk and did work that became torture in its repetitiveness. He willingly did this because that's what he had to do. He was a family man and he had a job, which was more than many people had. What his wife and kids didn't know was that John had been given his marchin' orders almost a month ago and would be officially jobless at the end of that day.

The morning walk to the subway was agony in its finality. He hated his job but had stuck with it and now he was at a difficult age; too young to retire and too old to find a new job. He had applied to dozens of jobs, phoned contacts he knew, even cold called some of the larger companies nearby, but no joy. Walkin' like a deadman, he headed to the bridge.

John stood at the rail for a very long time, watching the icy waters flow and feeling more helpless than he could ever remember. For him, this was it, his life was over. If he jumped, it would be sad for his family but he had a good life insurance policy and while he hadn't checked it for any suicide clauses, he wasn't in any mental condition to think things through so well.

Meanwhile back home, his wife, Debra, was preparing his favorite dinner and had baked him a cake. It was his birthday; he hadn't even remembered and, most likely, didn't care. Deb had invited a group of close friends and his children, who were growing up and could sometimes be awkward, were actually eager to surprise Dad.

For some reason, that only a *Jumper* might understand, John sat his briefcase near the old mesh screen, carefully folded his jacket and laid it over the railing. The bridge rarely had much foot traffic at this time of day and even less in such cold weather. John just stood, gazing at the small corner of the building that was just visible in the clustered skyline. The building where he'd worked for eighteen years. He turned and watched a couple of small tugboats chug beneath him and decided that as soon as the smallest one had passed under the bridge he would climb onto the rail and jump.

What John could not have known was that back at his home, where those who cared about him were waiting to wish him well, an old friend who had started a new business a year or two before was especially looking forward to his arrival. Doug Sherman was a successful guy, no doubt about it, but he had never changed from being a genuinely nice person and he wanted to offer John a job; a really great job.

Ya see, this is how the Lighthouse works. I am up here watchin' over everything and suddenly there is this SOS — urgent help needed — and I am here to help if I can. Remember, there is this Free Will thing that I told you about and sometimes there's not much I can do if it's part of someone's journey. Good or bad, it can't always be judged so easy.

Without delay, I get the spotlight revved up and turn the high-powered beam on Poor Tired John just as he's about to climb on that railing. Now I'm not one for givin' away trade secrets but just as John gets his leg over the top rail, a fella comes walkin' toward him and he's like the only other person on the bridge and nobody could'a seen him because, quite honestly, he wasn't there a second before. So, this fella doesn't walk too close to old Johnny boy because he doesn't want to spook him. He just smiles a really warm smile and calls out, *Hey buddy. Your phone's ringing!* You know, John's phone wasn't ringing but it was enough to cause him to climb back down, if just for a moment, and reach for his jacket just as his phone really did start to ring.

It was Debra, she was worried about him and said there was someone here who wanted to talk to him. As it happens, Doug Sherman was so excited about having John work with him that he took the phone from Deb and offered him the job right there and then. What could John say? Well, you know what he said and that's the importance of you all down in the City rememberin' that I'm here, in the Lighthouse all day every day and that, more times than not, I can do somethin' to help. Now it might not always be exactly what you want but most of the time it will be better and, okay, sometimes it might not be but that's generally because it's part of somethin' bigger yet to come.

John came close to makin' a bad choice and not only did life turn around for him in a way that exceeded his every dream but it also taught him not to despair or throw in the towel.

D'ya get it? Really? Great!

CHAPTER 9

Hiroshima

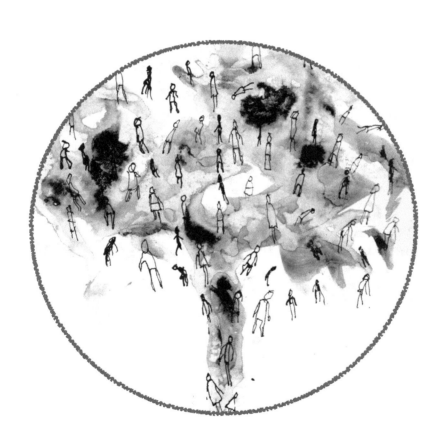

Do we think ... or should I say, *do you think* that committin' to an action which ends in pain or loss of life does not cause me to also feel pain or a sense of loss? If that were so, I wouldn't be takin' the time to talk with ya right now. By all that's holy — and that includes ALL that is — ya just can't justify the takin' of lives or the inflicting of sufferin' on other parts of the ALL and still think this won't affect you.

Here, come over near the window and sit. I need to find a way to make this work for ya. Say you had an ingrown toe nail and the entire toe caused you such discomfort that one day ya just decided to chop it off ... just chop it off with no consideration to whether it would hurt or not, or whether ya'd still be able ta walk properly, or even if the poor old toe itself might feel anything. I'm pretty sure ya wouldn't do such a stupid thing because you are connected enough to your toe, and other body parts, to understand that it's a bad idea and not least of all because of the pain ya know it's gonna cause. However, even just participatin' in any pain that's been caused to anything or anyone else in the ALL also involves you in a pain and has an impact that's just as real and far more detrimental than that poor toe of yours.

Now, believe it or not, even you pacifists who try to stand apart from war are as much involved as those who support violence in thought word or deed. Ya see, it ain't enough to divorce yourselves from the action of violence, or the belief in the need for violence, or in the necessity of violence. Ya actually need to step up and make it stop. Okay, now I hear ya and I know that it just ain't possible right now to make it stop and I know you're telling yourselves that at least you're keepin' peaceful and generatin' lovin' thoughts but it's not enough because *you are to the killing what the toe is to the body*, you are part of it even while passive.

Just for a minute, I want to talk about that first atom you all split and the niggardly way it was dropped on a nation of innocents and how it affected the ALL. In the first place, the energy in an atom — any atom — is proportionately equivalent to the speed at which it travels. However, because there is speed in all things on your planet and there is speed within the

particles of light that are, incidentally, not actually

moving toward you but — in fact — are remnants of

energy that's moving away from you, the force created

by this first atomic explosion was the force generated

when the energy and speed of matter came to a

standstill, which then turned back on your physical

universe. For one split moment, and I use the term split

very intentionally, you cracked the world in which you

live. Now, the universe — the ALL THAT IS - is stable

and knows no beginning and has no end, so nothin'

you do will end any-damned-thing. What your little

experiment did do was to effectively chop off the toe

of your very being and because you foolishly believed

it to be the other guy's toe, you were unable to feel the

immeasurable pain it caused and still causes.

Hiroshima was your foray into playing original

creator but because you already are part of the ALL

and the ALL is me and I am you, the most you could

do was to reverse the manifestation of energy and in

doing so, you robbed hundreds and thousands of souls

from experiencing their unique role in the

transfiguration of thought, which is energy, into matter,

which is physical life.

The learnin' from this experience has yet to take

place and largely due to the greed of those who are

dizzy with the brute force of what can be but must

never be, you are at a stalemate. Therefore, when I say

very truthfully that even the most passive amongst you are part of the violence, it is because you choose passivity out of fear and fear is another form of aggression and so it goes.

I sit up here wonderin' and worryin' more than you might imagine. I mean, there's billions of ya's down there all sharin' the same instinct for love and positivity which is exactly who I am ... I mean, I AM LOVE.

Okay, so now why the frown? You don't believe me? How can you not see yourself for what you are? I see, you find it hard to accept when there's so much hate and pain down there. I get it. I mean I really understand. Come on now, don't shake your head like that. Give me a moment and I will explain.

I was talkin' about Hiroshima and while I agree that you'd be right to think I took my eye off the ball on that one — and on quite a few other major events of mass destruction I hear you thinkin' — it's not because I do not love you. It's exactly BECAUSE I LOVE YOU that I have given you that freedom of choice. I admit, I was hopin' a whole lot more learnin' would have taken place but I know there are billions of ya's down there who are embracin' the message and maybe they seem small in the face of so much that's bad. I can promise you that things are gonna change.

Here's the thing; ya see, like I said, there are billions of souls here who one would think lost their lives too soon or too unfairly and probably even catastrophically. And I can hear ya thinkin' of the Holocaust and I am gonna answer that when you're ready to hear it. For now, let's just say that while there seems no answer to events that result in a catastrophic loss of lives, you need to believe me when I say that these souls will be in a better position to bring peace when they return.

What? Yea of course ya return and if ya want Buddha to text ya a second opinion to confirm that, I'd be happy to arrange it. Okay, so stick with me here and I'll try to explain.

When a soul is ripped from the physical in an event that is fueled by hatred and anger, they come here in a state that is both confused and frightened. It's a major undertaking to soothe these individuals and get them to a place where they can feel the divine love which surrounds them. Yea, you're right, it's a time of healin' and for some it happens quickly while for others it can take a very long time.

I'm gonna tell you a story now, about a young girl named Shula. She was what ya might call a survivor but ya need to understand why it was more than just physical.

CHAPTER 10

The Tale of Shula

Now, I understand how this is a delicate and very painful subject. It is painful for me as I am everything that is, was, or ever will be, and within me lives all pain as well as all joy. So, I am respectin' both the pain and the joy within this story of Shula.

This is not the place for me to go into the deep dark energies behind the Nazis and their desire to exterminate an entire race of people. It is part of Shula's story but it is not the part I need to share now.

When the new regime came to power, many Jewish people were frightened, as they had the right to be, and many had wisely already left their homes. However, there were those who had such a deep connection that they could not bring themselves to leave. Shula was a young girl when the Nazis took over and she had two aging parents to care for. In the town where they lived, she was surrounded by connections of such emotional depth that this gave her a strong sense of identity. The buildings, the schools, the cemetery, were all places where members of her family had left a mark.

Shula came from an important and well respected family. They were originally from Poland but had long ago moved to Munich so to take advantage of the demand for skilled carpenters and weavers and such like.

Munich was what you might call an enlightened city and it was where Shula was born. Her family was large and they were well educated. Due to certain restrictions of a political nature, Shula and her parents focused on running their shop. They offered ornamental furniture which was made by her father and uncle while the women made beautiful hand woven fabrics. This worked well for the family for many years and Munich was a good place for them. However, shopkeeping was not their only trade and behind the scenes of this quiet little shop, they produced religious items; some of the most beautiful items for the Holy Of Holies - the most sacred place of the Hebrew Temple, ya see.

These items were created and crafted with such a deep love of God and the traditions of the Jewish people that they were doubly blessed; firstly through the intense devotion of Shula's family, who dedicated their skills and secondly, by the high Rabbi of the synagogue.

Ya need ta realize that the Jewish faith was basically just about tolerated and because of this the Jewish Ghettos were the places where most Germans and most Christians did not want to venture. The Jews encouraged this. They contributed to the outer areas of their communities in a way that almost encouraged it to look schmatte — ya know, shabby. But I can tell ya right now, within these communities there were treasures and wealth that even many working class Jews knew little about. It was in the Synagogue, for the most part, that the wealth and the sacred treasures were kept. I can tell ya that if ya could'a taken a bird's eye view of any of these few ghetto neighborhoods ya would'a always found the temple near the center. *Let things that are pure stand protected behind the schmatte* was a phrase ya might hear if ya were Jewish and if ya were young and if ya ever asked why.

Well, Shula was one of those young Jews who did ask. She was only trying to help and when she asked her momma why she couldn't dress up the shop windows a bit — just a little — to maybe display some of the fine craftsmanship, her mother pulled her to one side and, grabbing her by the ear, she said, *I've told you, Shula. Let those things that are pure be kept behind the schmatte.*

Then she whispered with a foreboding intensity, *Things are changing here and you need to be like the rats; going about your business in quiet ways and in places they won't care to go.*

Of course, Shula's mother was referring to the new Republic that was gaining power and she knew, she could really sense, what was coming.

Again, because Shula was young, she didn't understand just what the Nazis would be capable of and somehow she just thought of her mother as old fashioned and a worrier. In her young, creative mind, she thought that if any of the new police came by and saw the beauty of their wares, they would understand what an asset her family was to Germany.

When Shula's parents returned home and saw

what their girl had done to the window display they

were furious but more than that, they were frightened.

With no explanation, they packed a small case for their

daughter, shoved her paperwork in the pocket of her

jacket and marched her down the street to an uncle's

home.

Take her with, Janisch, please. It's not safe. Her uncle

put his arm around the girl and pulled her near.

Turning to his wife he said, *It's time.*

We will follow, I promise. her mother cried, trying to

kiss Shula as her husband dragged her away.

Shula's parent's never had time to pack. Her

mother was lighting the stump of a candle and her

father had just turned the lock on the door when the Nazi police kicked it in.

Shula was fortunate. Along with her aunt and uncle, she travelled to France where they gained passage on a boat to New York.

Shula studied hard and became a teacher and a writer; a very beautiful writer of poetry and an advocate for freedom, especially as it spoke of religious freedom. Sadly, she did not see her parents again but she never forgot how they gave their lives so she could know freedom.

In fact, she's on one of the upper floors right now doin' the same work she did down there. Sure, she still writes but now she uses a kind of loving energy that just goes out there with her words and these messages

sometimes take root with a young girl who might

suddenly have an amazing flash of inspiration. So, ya

see, that's another reason why you can't never think

you're alone because it just ain't so.

CHAPTER 11

Robert Writes A Best Seller

It was maybe a few years ago, down there in a real busy part of the city, when I spotted Robert - he was an editor for one of the really big publishing houses, working on his own first novel. I mean he believed in this book like I can't begin to tell ya and it was all he could do ta not pack it all in and go live in some shelter somewhere just so he could write. Sure, I knew it was a great book because I can feel these things — the really great things that all of ya's create or try to create. Don't get me wrong, all creative efforts are great if you judge them by love, passion and commitment but not everyone trusts themselves enough to really allow the highest and best to flow through. Not so with Robert. He was the book, as they say, and he was so open that it was just a matter of time before he'd be a famous published writer.

Well, he did find it damned difficult reviewin' and editing manuscripts from writers that he knew were not that great; writers that he knew he was better than, but he was not that kind of guy… not the type that belittles other people, even mentally. Still, he found it very hard to sit there at that desk, with his red pencil and his green pencil and his blue pencil, goin' over manuscript and press sheets all day long. The thing that made it even worse was his boss, Simon, who was, if I dare say it, an asshole. He rode his employees like the devil he was and it was no different at home; he treated his poor wife like she was an idiot and only seemed to find a use for her when it was time to parade her in front of clients and friends. She was beautiful and he knew it, and so did she but her beauty was not something she gave much importance to. Her name was Barbra. She was the office manager when she first met Simon. At first, because she really did love him, it seemed a romantic and supportive decision to give up her job and stay at home with the plan being to raise a family. Sadly, the kids never came along and when it was discovered by the doctor that the problem was not with young Barbra but with Simon, everything changed. Somehow, her husband twisted the facts into such a tool of torment that she actually began to believe that she had caused her husband's infertility.

He began to beat her fairly regularly but never around the face because she was still that beautiful trophy that he loved to dangle from his arm.

Well, as time passed, Barbra became more and more depressed and try as she may, it was becoming more and more difficult for her to remain focused on her role as wife to Simon. Did her husband notice or even care? Hell no, if anything, her sadness just made him treat her worse. Now, what Barbra or anyone else did not know about Simon was that he also longed to be a writer but, unlike Robert, he didn't have the inner fire to do anything about it, other than to quietly let it fester inside.

Are ya keeping up with me here? Ya are? Good.

Well, as it happened, Robert actually trusted Simon.

He respected him as a boss and they were both

working toward the same goal which was to publish

best-selling books. So, one autumn day, Robert decides

to ask Simon if he'd mind reading his novel. A bigger

dumb decision ya don't never see too often, but that's

what he did. Now Simon, who was a deeply disturbed

and frustrated closet-author, was knocked over

sideways by the manuscript. It was the best novel he

had ever read. It was so good, that he wished he had

written it himself. One thought led to another and it

didn't take much for him to create a self-delusional

reality where he actually was the author. So, Simon

goes directly to his boss and humbly asks, *I know you're busy but it would mean a great deal if you could take a look at this novel I've been working on. Sure, of course I write,* he said as convincingly as any bastard had ever lied before, *I just wanted to wait until I had something that might be worth sharing.* So, his boss agreed to look at the typewritten manuscript and actually told Simon that he liked his initiative. Like I said, the guy was a bastard. Well, as you have probably already guessed, his boss loved the book, in fact he loved it so much that it was all the executives could talk about; you know, their new Best Seller. Robert couldn't believe what was happening but when he challenges his bastard of a boss, he is instantly dismissed and marched out'a the building.

I kid you not, this was like somethin' from a movie. Imagine Robert standin' outside of the revolving door to one of the world's biggest publishers, bent over pickin' up his papers, his coat, and other personal belongings that had been tossed out behind him. He hadn't even had time to become truly angry.

Well, Robert was a nice guy, he really was, so he dusted himself off, went home and sent a few resumes to some other publishers. This guy had a good reputation and it wasn't long before he landed a new job; maybe not as well paying as the one he'd just left but at least there wasn't any Simon.

Now, I've told ya before that the City has a strange and perfect way of keepin' things in balance and Robert's case was no exception. As Robert was settling into his new editor job, Barbra had made the decision that she could not stand being stuck home every day and while she wasn't at the point of leaving Simon, she had decided to get a job and didn't give a damn what he might say or try to do about it. Well, in the spirit of keeping things balanced, I felt this overwhelming urge to step in and sort of help influence events — just a little — so she could land a job at the same place as Robert; in fact the same department if you don't mind holdin' the applause 'til the end.

Simon's stolen book was on track to become a best seller; all of the prepublication reviews said so.

However, I knew different and events were just waitin'
for the right moment to unfold. You might be askin'
why Robert didn't put up a fight and why he didn't
have another copy. Firstly, he wasn't aggressive like that
and, secondly, he did have a second copy but it was
gone. Ya see, he was not without an ego and he did
wonder what someone else might think, so, quite a few
months previous to all of the Simon stuff, he had asked
his neighbor, who actually was a published author, if
he might take a look. Like I said, this was a good few
months before he'd lost his job and while other things
were happenin', the neighbor just moved away. It
never occurred to Robert to try tracking the guy down
and, without another copy of the book, that was more

or less the reason he didn't feel strong enough to fight the fight.

Okay, confused? Hold on because it gets better. Robert has no idea that Barbra is married to his old devil boss but he does feel an attraction to her and she likes him, too. She thinks he's kind and smart. He thinks she is gentle and beautiful. Oh boy, I think this was one of my best interventions ever.

It was about 7 am on a Monday morning when Robert gets a phone call from his old neighbor, Sam. He wants to apologize about the book. *I forgot all about it*, he says, *and it wasn't until I read some of the extracts in the Times Review that it seemed familiar.* So, Robert goes on to explain all the shit he'd been through and Sam offers to bring the only other copy over that evening. Not only does he bring the other manuscript but he is accompanied by his own attorney who specializes in — you guessed it — publishing law. On Tuesday morning, Robert is feeling so happy that he asks Barbra out to lunch, during which date he tells her about the book and she realizes what her husband has done. Barbra tearfully confesses the connection but Robert is already so enraptured, he doesn't even care. By this point, he is holding her hand and she is holding his. On Wednesday morning, Robert and Sam's lawyer show up unannounced at Simon's office with a copy of the original manuscript only they don't want to see him, they are there to see his boss. Then, comes Thursday morning and Robert tells Barbra how he feels and she smiles and says she feels the same. He explains what has happened and that he has a meeting with his old employer who is now his new publisher and does she want to leave work early and come with.

Well, I get all tingly just tellin' ya this story but the long and short of it is that on Thursday afternoon, Robert and Barbra pull up to his old work address and new publisher on Park Avenue where they are greeted by a valet who says he will park their car. R and B step toward a smiling doorman just as poor jobless lying Simon is being thrown through the same open door and out onto the pavement, followed by his briefcase, a few fluttering papers, and a rolled-up overcoat.

CHAPTER 12

Everyone Is Beautiful

Now I promise ya when I say this … and it's not just me tryin' to be idealistic; every one of ya's are beautiful, full stop, not open for debate. On top of that, ya need to accept that every creature, plant, living thing right down to the microbes that ya can't see are also beautiful. This is not some kind a new age gambit I'm pullin' here but something I just really need ya's ta embrace; and here's why.

Amy was a very special young girl. She had been born without a face; at least not a face the way most of ya think. So, without going into explicit detail, I will just say that she did not have a face. She was raised by truly loving parents and these folks loved her without hesitation. Her beauty was expressed in so many other ways that I'm thinkin' ya might feel uncomfortable if I shared my true admiration.

As a baby, she was bright; very bright. Her parents had tried for so long to have children that when she was born — in fact, before she was born — they had chosen her name, Amy, which means beloved. Few children, even those born perfect in every way, were loved more than Amy and maybe that is why she grew up with this remarkable ability to love and see the good in everyone.

Her first few years were perfect. It was difficult for her mother having to explain to the other moms about the physical issues with her baby but Amy could see, she could make sounds, she could eat — with some difficulty — and she could smile, but it wasn't a smile like most of you would recognize. When Amy smiled, she smiled with her eyes, which sort of grew wider and turned up a bit at the sides. It was at those smiling moments that the light inside of this child would really shine and folks had to get to know her before they appreciated the magic of the light that came from within this girl. I can honestly say that I don't think Amy ever felt unloved … until she started school.

Everyone knows that children can be mean; they can be down right cruel. It's always bothered me because I so often get those painful prayers from a heart that has been damaged and Amy's was one of the most heartfelt pleas I have ever heard.

Please, dear God. Please, can't you make me like the other kids. Can't you make me pretty like the girls at school. Please? I promise to never be bad, ever.

It tore at me deep inside and I'm the one who keeps tellin' ya that there's a reason for everything and that nobody is born down in that City without havin' agreed to whatever they've taken on. Amy was no exception but that beautiful light and her kindness and her loving heart called out to me like nothin' I've ever known. I admit, I took a special interest in this child and as she grew up, it became harder and harder for me to watch her deal with so many challenges and so much cruelty.

All was not lost, thankfully, and as Amy became a young teen, she learned to rise above the meanness and to ignore those types of people, which included a good many grownups, I hate to say. She was quiet, because talkin' wasn't easy, but she did make a few friends; and they were true friends who helped guide Amy through some difficult stuff. Can ya imagine how she felt approaching adolescence and findin' herself interested in boys? It was brutal and she was so filled with inner turmoil and frustration that I stayed very near to her for a good year or so and did whatever I could. Ultimately, it wasn't anything I did that helped Amy as much as that incredible light of hers.

Amy was not the only kid in her school with challenges, although she had more than most, there was also this boy that everyone called *Freddy the Freak,* except Amy; she called him Frederick because he told her that was his real name and he preferred it. Amy and Frederick became close and maybe it was because he wasn't perfect either. Ya see, Frederick told Amy he had a sick heart and that was why he had to take things easy and not exert himself. So, while lots of the other kids picked on him, Amy found herself being protective and she surrounded her dear Frederick with so much light, the two of them absolutely glowed.

It was the afternoon that Frederick asked her to the school dance and said he wanted to take her because she was beautiful that Amy knew she loved him. Ya might say a couple of fifteen year old kids can't fall in love, but these two had been through some

serious stuff and I could see that what they were feelin'
was real.

The night of the dance was magical. Frederick
bought Amy a flower for her dress and she gave him a
carnation for his jacket. During the final dance, there
was a light surrounding the two of them that cast the
most beautiful aura. Everyone must have sensed it
because they stopped dancin' and just watched.

As the music ended, Frederick pulled Amy close
and kissed her and while it was a bit clumsy, neither of
them cared. Frederick whispered, *I love you*, and she
said, *ditto*. A moment later, Frederick fell to the floor,
short of breath, his arms folded on his chest. At the

hospital, the doctors shared their opinion that things did not look good.

Frederick was not allowed to go home and he continued to get weaker. Amy tried to stay positive and never lost hope. She sat with him every day and talked about their future and their plans; she wanted to be brave because part of her believed it would really help.

Amy had just said goodnight to Frederick and decided she wanted to walk home. She needed to think and she wanted to talk to me in that way I had come to know as uniquely hers. I was listenin' to every word and maybe because of that I wasn't watchin' out for her the way I usually did. Ya see, Amy had never been able to cry; not once in her entire life had she shed a single tear so it was almost more than I could handle

when I sensed those tears falling from her eyes. My

greatest love was surrounding her and her pain was my

pain. Maybe it was because the tears affected her

vision, which wasn't great at the best of times, that she

stepped out in front of that car.

In the hospital she said she wanted Frederick to

have her heart. *Please mom, I love him. He has it already.*

This way I can be with him forever. She smiled that crinkled

smile of hers then left her body to come here with me.

Now, you can go ahead and say it was against the odds,

but Amy's heart was a good match for Frederick and

he did regain his health. In time, he met someone else.

They fell in love and married but never did he forget

Amy; he could feel her love beatin' in his chest every minute of every day. When he and his wife had their first child, they named her Amy, who was perfect and beautiful and loved so very much.

CHAPTER 13

Estercraft

We all need love; it's a fact. Even if ya do not believe me, ya can see the painful effects of non-love all around ya's. Sure, I thought ya'd say that and I don't blame ya. You're right, people do have a funny way of showin' it and the world don't seem to be in such a bad way for any lack of it. Well, NEWS FLASH, I'm tellin' ya right now, the world is in a bad way for the lack of love and I've got another true story that's just perfect for illustratin' what I mean.

Estercraft was a gypsy; a true Romani gypsy. She was born with the gift; ya know, the gift of second sight. With her extended family, she travelled all around Europe and the more she saw the more she hurt — deep inside. It was kinda like she was takin' on the pain and sorrows of others, which was never her intention. In fact, she had been taught by her grandmother, her own mother and even her aunties, about the ways to avoid takin' on bad energies. Then why was she feelin' so sick and so sad all of the time? Well, I'll tell ya; it was because she cared … she really cared and maybe just a little too much did she care.

Now, I could relate to Estercraft because she was a whole lot like me in the way she was takin' on the pains and sufferin' of others but, unlike me, she couldn't process it … ya know, cleanse herself of it, and that's not good.

Every village these Gypsies stopped in, Ester was like a magnet and the sick were drawn to her — or she was drawn to them. Little children especially resonated with her and she just followed what her inner senses told her, which was to heal. So imagine, years and years of sharing the gift of healing with hundreds, maybe thousands, of folks who needed her gifts. No, not everyone was healed in the way you might consider the meaning of the word, but they all found themselves at peace with their illness and were able to pass without fear; and I'm gonna talk about healing a bit more if ya can hang around long enough.

Anyway, the call came to me when Ester had almost reached breakin' point and that's when I focused my attention and turned the old light up there full-on to this young woman who was carryin' the pain of so many people. What could I do? I mean it's against the ways of the City to just somehow wave my arms and cleanse her - that wouldn'ta been right, ya understand. So, I got her into my focus and could see, almost immediately, that she was on the verge of gettin' sick inside; real sick.

Damn, it was difficult — a real big problem — ya know what I mean? She wasn't lettin' the negative energy wash over her the way she shoulda been doin'; the way her mother and grandmother had taught her and, now that she was sick, they were strugglin' to get through to her so she could get well. I knew this wasn't her time to die — not her rightful time — and somehow I needed to play interference and finesse some powerful solution but fast.

My challenge was in gettin' through to her without showin' myself.

What's that? I do that all of the time? Hey, you're a smart cookie! Yea, I do show myself a lot, it's true, but it's showin' my love without givin' away my presence ... that's the tricky part.

So, in the case of dear sweet Estercraft, I had decided to direct some phenomenal healing her way and I can't say that this was because she was more deservin' than anybody else because that would be incorrect and unfair to the rest of ya's.

I do not like cancer. Yea, you heard me right; I do not like cancer and it ain't one of them things I would be okay with if it wasn't for you all and your free will.

Yes and no ... I did create everything but everything is forever changin' and because you are part of me and we are all part of an eternal give-and-take there are things that happen which I cannot say are strictly the product of love. Sorry kid, but that's the way it is. Sadly, cancer is one of them things and in the case of dear Ester, she needed my help.

Okay, I hear ya — why should she get a miracle when so many of the rest of ya's do not and that's not an easy one to answer. For some of ya the work you need to do is best finished in another way, in a way that no longer involves being a physical individual. Yea, that's right; ya got it — because most of them folks have finished what they went to the City to do and need to move on to continue learnin' and growin' in a different way. Yea, it does seem unfair and I'm goin' ta chew on my thoughts for a while before I attempt an answer. For now, I can only say, it's complicated. Okay?

Well, gettin' back to Ester, I knew that, despite her colorful gypsy upbringing, she had some very strong religious beliefs that were both a help and a hindrance to her. Just as I was formulatin' a solution, the poor kid slipped into a coma and I thought we were gonna lose her. She was sick; very sick and to tell ya the truth, I was very tempted to let her come back here and stay awhile in this here Lighthouse, but I could see that she was creatin' this scenario on her own because she really did believe that selfless love equalled deep and painful suffering. As soon as I picked up that connection, it was all the justification I needed to turn up the healing lights and bring her back.

While she was in that deep, deep sleep of hers, she came to see me and I admit I was a bit surprised that she had those resources but she was an angel, she really was, and she followed her heart which led her back home ... so this is what I did.

We walked. We walked through that door over there and on the other side there was a garden and it was the kind of garden that not only provided some much needed healing to our Estercraft but it was also a place that reminded her of her physical home and how much love she still had to give.

We walked and she talked and I listened. I held her hand and I gave her my healing love. The garden became a forest and the forest grew dark. Ester faced her greatest fears and she cried; she really cried. I put my arm around her and walked her to that place where the forest ends and the light returns and at the end of that walk she found her way back to her family. I gave her a smile and a little bit of a nudge and when she opened her eyes, she was healed.

Without goin' into the great complicated details, because it's only gonna confuse ya, I can only say that every one of ya's has unique issues and every issue has its special solution. Ester was no different. She was afraid. She was afraid of failing and of not being strong enough to do what her heart told her, which was to help and to heal.

Now, not many folks would guess that the Romani Gypsies are a very traditional people when it comes to religion and they sometimes walk that wavy line between natural magic and organized christianity — and that's okay. It's not always about the truth, because the truth is vast; sometimes it's more about what a person believes is the truth which is enough to get them by. So, in the case of Estercraft, she said goodbye to her mother, father and family at the door of The Sacred Heart Convent. She took her vows, turned her back on the world she had known, and took the name of Sister Mary Craft. Her healing energy and loving light has been a real blessing to so many. I think of her often and, just like I care for the rest of ya's, there's a dedicated space in my heart where I follow her on her journey. Sure, there's a whole lot that you and most other folks can learn from her story ... but I'll stop there and leave you to meditate on it.

CHAPTER 14

Home Is Where Your Heart Is

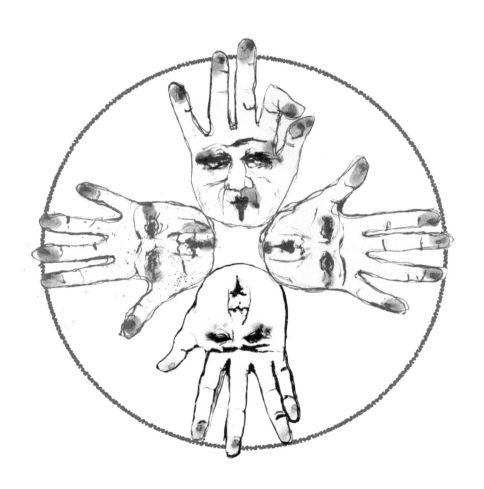

Now, I'm sittin' here lookin' at ya and talkin' to ya … and I'm doin' most of the talkin' and you're not sayin' much of anything. Yea, I know, I talk too much sometimes and I gotta work on that. Understand, I don't get many visitors and I especially do not get visitors with such a beautiful energy as what you have.

So now, I'm gonna shut my big mouth for a bit and just listen. If ya just wanna sit quite, we can do quiet. If ya wanna leave, I guess that's okay too.

What's that? Sleepin' … me? I don't never sleep and while I know it might'a looked that way, I was actually workin'. Remember, omnipotent, as in everywhere at once and that kind'a thing? Anyway, you were sayin' that you were sort'a thinkin' about goin' home. I gotta tell ya that you really are home so just relax and let me explain.

Ya see, when you first arrived, I knew why ya were here. I could feel it emanatin' from ya like the rays of the sun. You felt confused and lost and I don't blame ya. It ain't easy when a guy like you finds himself on an elevator that just goes one way.

Are you dead? Mmm … good question. Do ya feel dead?

I'm sorry, kid. Come on, please don't go berserk on me. If ya let the fear kick in I'm gonna lose ya and I don't wanna' be sendin' out no search parties just when things are goin' so well.

Okay. Good. That's it, relax and just try to listen.

That word, death, is so damned full of

negativity and fear that I don't blame ya for freakin'

out. But, the truth is that the very thing you fear is a

life that's truly alive. It's a doorway and a return to

your true home.

I do not want any of ya's to fear this thing ya

call death. There's nothin' to be afraid of, I promise

you.

Do I look dead? Is the energy you're feelin' here

now, with me, life-less?

So, what are you feelin'?

Exactly, you feel rested, at peace, safe, and …

well, alive.

Welcome home, kid.

The truth is, you don't ever really leave; you just shift focus and take some time out to learn. The City is your homeschoolin', as it were, and I would be lyin' if I said it was meant to be easy. But, oh what a feeling of bliss when you return.

My love is with you, always, and the others — the ones ya had dinner with when ya first arrived — they took the same journey that you've been on and came home wiser and stronger and more fearless than it might seem possible.

Ya see, you don't have nothin' to fear for this is your life and your life is forever.

Well, okay, you're right; I guess I am sort of ramblin'. What I'm tryin' to say is that you will have countless journeys in your experience and because

consciousness is eternal and life is everlasting, there's

only one thing that matters.

You got it; LOVE - and learning how powerful

and how important it is in everything you have done or

will ever do.

Well, you came back now because … well,

because you were finished … for the time being.

Sure you feel tired. Life in the City is exhausting

and there ain't no other place like it, trust me. Like we

used to say, way back when:

Om Asato Maa Sad-Gamaya.

From the unreal lead us to the real.

Tamaso Maa Jyotir Gamaya.

From darkness lead us to Light.

Mrityor-Maa Amrtam Gamaya.

From death lead us to Immortality.

Om Shaantih, Shaantih, Shaantih.

Aum Peace, Peace, Peace.

There's more to it; much more … but for now,

you should rest … just rest.

OTHER BOOKS by Tobias Inigo

DOGS of FAMOUS ARTISTS

SMALL GARDENS
12 landscape designs for small spaces

GURU

THE GOD CLOUD (by Anonymous)

Available at:

http://www.lulu.com   - search Tobias Inigo

or contact the author at tobiasart.com